MY
GIRLY UNICORN

ISBN # 978-0-9627436-3-4

Far, faraway in magical clouds so high,
a rainbow shone in a cotton-candy sky.

1.

**The air was sweetened with a sugar cube twist,
while unicorns played in a gumdrop mist.**

**Inside the rainbow, a field was set for fun,
and all of the unicorns' work had been done.**

3.

**But in the field, at the sad and lonely end,
a girl unicorn played without a single friend.**

4.

She danced her dance in the bright sunlight, practicing all day, so she could get it right.

Other unicorns called her all kinds of names,
and wouldn't pick her for any of their games.

**They made fun of her big hair and purple horn,
always calling her "_That_ Girly Unicorn."**

7.

When the other unicorns were bored and dared to explore,
they passed through the rainbow's multi-colored door. 8.

They raced down the rainbow's beam to the ground,
and their bumpy landing made an awful sound.

9.

That Girly Unicorn went at her own pace, knowing she would lose this midair race.

**Other unicorns laughed as they passed her by,
leaving her alone to only ask "Why?"**

As they played without her, she became quite sad,
wondering what she had done that was so bad.

Then, an evil darkness filled the sky throughout,
and playtime for all was now in serious doubt.

13.

**Vicious rain clouds growled like a hungry bear,
as lightning bolts shot throughout the stormy air.**

14.

The other unicorns were frightened and scared,
crying for help from anyone who cared.

15.

They searched for the rainbow's shiny beam,
without any luck, or so it would seem.

16.

"Your rainbow is gone!" An angry rain cloud hissed.
The last chance to get home had been barely missed.

Slowly they tried to fly away, one by one.
But lightning stopped their flight before it'd begun.

**Floodwaters circled and trapped the unicorns so tight.
Their days were numbered, 'cause no help was in sight.**   **19.**

One unicorn cried, "No hope, we are all done."
Alas, the fields were flooded, no place to run.

20.

Then, the unicorns heard a noise in the night,
"Splash, Splash, Step left, Splash, Splash, Step right."

They moved closer to this odd and strange sound, hoping it would help and lead to drier ground.

22.

It was _That_ Girly Unicorn and her dance, remembering her steps as if by chance.

A ray of sunlight twinkled as it broke through,
and the other unicorns' hopes grew and grew.

24.

**But rain clouds kept firing lightning bolts to fill the sky,
stopping the ray of sunlight on its very first try.** 25.

"Stop that dance!" was the rain clouds' powerful plea.
"It's hurting our storm, as anyone can see."

26.

Yet the dance continued without a delay.
That Girly Unicorn's dance became a ballet.

"We're shrinking!" The rain clouds said with a loud weep.
"And we're so tired. It's putting us to sleep."

28.

The dance became faster with hooves two by two,
while the rain clouds shrank as they became so few!

Rays of sunlight cracked through the clouds so tiny.
The rainbow appeared, and was oh so shiny!

**The other unicorns had one thing to say,
for treating _That_ Girly Unicorn _that_ way.**

**Each one waited for her to come into view,
shouting, "_My_ Girly Unicorn! I LOVE YOU!**

VISIT US AT:

WWW.MYGIRLYUNICORN.COM